Dead Wood

Andy Croft

A & C Black • London

First published 2012 by A & C Black,
an imprint of Bloomsbury Publishing Plc
50 Bedford Square, London WC1B 3DP

www.acblack.com

Copyright © 2012 Andy Croft
Illustrations copyright © 2012 Sean Longcroft

The rights of Andy Croft and Sean Longcroft to be identified
as the author and illustrator of this work have been asserted by them
in accordance with the Copyrights, Designs and Patents Act 1988.

ISBN 978-1-4081-6335-1

A CIP catalogue for this book is available from the British Library.

This book is produced using paper that is made from wood
grown in managed, sustainable forests. It is natural, renewable
and recyclable. The logging and manufacturing processes conform
to the environmental regulations of the country of origin.

Printed by CPI Group (UK), Croydon, CR0 4YY

recommended by

www.catchup.org

Catch Up is a not-for-profit charity
which aims to address the problem of
underachievement that has its roots in
literacy and numeracy difficulties.

DEAD WOOD

For Arthur

Contents

Chapter One   Orchard View   7

Chapter Two   Holly   14

Chapter Three   Ash   23

Chapter Four   Willow   32

Chapter Five   Timber!   44

Chapter Six   Roots   56

Chapter One

Orchard View

Holly knew there were ghosts in this house. There had to be. There were always ghosts in old houses. And this was the oldest house she had ever seen.

The old brick walls were thick with ivy. The garden was full of weeds. Some of the roof tiles were missing and the downstairs windows had boards on them. The old house had been empty for years, but now they were going to live in it.

Wicked!

Holly's dad worked for a firm of builders. They had bought the house and the old orchard to build some new houses on the land. The estate was going to be called 'Orchard View'.

Holly's dad was the site manager, so they were all going to live in the old house until the new houses were built.

Holly was into ghosts. She loved ghost stories. When she was younger, her favourite film was *Caspar*, then *Ghostbusters*. Now it was *The Ring*.

Holly wasn't scared of ghosts. She liked the idea that the dead were still around. So far, the only ghosts she had seen were on the ghost-train at a seaside fun-fair. But she was sure there must be a ghost in this old house.

While the removal men unloaded their things, Holly helped her dad remove the boards from the windows. The kitchen table was still in the van, so they ate a picnic tea on the kitchen floor. Then Holly decided to explore the house.

She went up the first staircase. It led to the first-floor landing and the big bedrooms. A smaller staircase led to more bedrooms on the top floor.

She went up the stairs and tried to switch on the lights but some of them didn't work. It was starting to get dark outside.

Creepy!

The top landing was cold and damp and covered in dust. There were cobwebs everywhere. Holly pushed at a door, and it swung open with a slow and painful creak. Inside the room, everything was covered in dust sheets.

There was a door at the end of the corridor. Perhaps it led to the attic. Holly tried the handle, but it was locked. She turned round to go back downstairs. And then she saw her.

At the far end of the corridor was a dark shape. A young girl, about Holly's age and height, standing looking at her. Holly's heart was beating fast. She could hear herself breathing. She told herself that there was nothing to be scared of.

Slowly she stepped towards the girl. The girl moved towards her.

Holly stopped dead. So did the girl. Holly smiled. So did the girl. Then they both started laughing. It was just an old mirror!

Chapter Two

Holly

The next day Holly was woken by the sound of shouting outside her window. There was a crowd of people in front of the house.

Some of them were carrying signs. One of them was talking through a loudspeaker.

They were clapping their hands and chanting, "Save our trees! Save our trees!"

She found her mum and dad eating breakfast in the kitchen.

"Who are all those people?" she asked. "What do they want?"

Her dad put down his coffee. "They are from the village," he said. "They want to save the trees in the orchard."

"But haven't you chopped most of them down?" asked Holly.

"We have," said her dad, grinning. "The last ones come down on Monday, and then we'll start building the estate."

"It's a bit silly calling it Orchard View," said Holly. "There won't be any orchard left."

"It's just a name," her mum said. "It will be a lot nicer round here when all those old trees have gone. They give me the creeps."

"It's those tree-huggers that give me the creeps," her dad said. "Don't they have anything better to do than make a fuss about trees?"

Through the window Holly could see a tall girl with silver hair climbing one of the old trees. The shouting outside was getting louder.

"They sound upset," Holly said.

"I will be upset if they don't go away soon," said her dad. "This is private land!"

BANG!

Something hit the window. The crowd were throwing stones at the house.

"Right!" shouted Holly's dad. "I've had enough of this."

He stormed out of the kitchen and went to shout at the protestors. They kept on chanting, "Save our trees! Save our trees!"

Holly slipped out of the back door and ran round the house. She joined the crowd just as her dad was yelling that he'd called the police.

"Save our trees! Save our trees!" shouted the crowd again

The trees in the old orchard swayed in the wind, as if they were joining in the protest.

"Hi," said a voice above her.

Holly looked up. It was the tall girl with silver hair. She was sitting on a tree branch.

"I'm Ash," said the girl, jumping down.

"I'm Holly."

"I know. You've moved into the old house. And that must be your dad," Ash said, pointing to Holly's dad, who was waving his arms about like a tree in a gale.

Holly pulled a face. "Dad's OK, really. But this job is stressing him out. The houses have to be built by Christmas. So they need to cut down the rest of the trees."

Ash frowned. "I know people need houses. But people need trees too. This orchard has been here for ever. There used to be all kinds of fruit trees here. Apples, cherries, plums and pears. An old lady lived here before you, and she used to talk to the trees in the orchard."

Just then a tall, thin boy came up to them. Ash smiled at him.

"This is my big brother," she said to Holly.

"Hi," said the boy, giving Holly a big smile. He had green eyes, like Ash. "My name's Willow, but everyone calls me Will."

"That's funny," said Holly. "All our names are the names of trees. Holly, Ash and Willow."

But it didn't matter what he was called. He was the best-looking boy she had ever seen.

Chapter Three

Ash

A couple of weeks later Holly's dad had
to go to London for a big meeting. Her mum
was going with him.

Dad was even more stressed than usual. The protestors had tied themselves to the trees to stop him from cutting them down. The police had arrested four people in the end.

Then Holly's dad had chopped down the last trees, but the new houses were still not built. The builders had lost time, and time meant money. And money was all her mum and dad seemed to care about.

Her parents had told her to avoid the protestors. But she liked Ash. And she really liked Will. So she didn't tell her parents that Ash was coming for a sleep-over while they were away.

After her parents had gone, Holly showed
her new friend round the house.

"It's amazing!" said Ash. "It's so old."

Holly showed her the two staircases and
the bathroom with the old-fashioned bath.

Ash laughed when Holly pointed out the mirror where she thought she had seen a ghost.

Later they sat munching pizza and watching an old DVD of *Ghost*. Holly tried to imagine Will dying and coming back to look after her, like in the film.

"Do you think this house is really haunted?" asked Ash.

"I don't know. I hope so," said Holly.

Ash laughed. "Aren't you scared of ghosts?"

"It's only in stories that ghosts are scary," said Holly. "If there is a ghost in this house it will be the old lady. I am sure she is friendly.

Maybe she will come out tonight. Touch wood..."

They took sleeping-bags up to the attic. Holly thought a ghost might walk around up there. They sat up for hours, eating sweets and telling ghost stories. Outside the wind was whipping round the old house. It was a perfect setting for a ghost story. But there was no sign of a ghost.

Suddenly the lights went out. Both girls screamed.

"What's happened?" whispered Holly.

"Must be a fuse," said Ash. "Do you know where the fuse box is?"

"The what?" asked Holly.

"Never mind," Ash said. "Are there any candles?"

There were some candles somewhere, but Holly didn't know where they were kept. She wasn't going to start looking for them in the dark.

She wanted to ring her mum and dad but she had left her phone downstairs.

BANG!

The girls jumped. Someone was knocking very loudly on the front door.

"Do you think we should see who it is?" asked Ash.

"There is no way I'm going downstairs!" said Holly.

"But it could be important," said Ash.

"At one o'clock in the morning?" Holly asked.

"Maybe it's the police," Ash said.

"The police?" Holly suddenly felt afraid.

Then they heard it. Someone – or something – was tapping on the window.

"What is it?" whispered Holly. "I'm scared."

Outside they could hear the wind howling. The knocking sound was getting louder.

Then the sound changed. The banging was now *inside* the house.

The floorboards were creaking. It sounded as if someone was coming up the stairs.

The tapping on the window grew louder and louder.

"What are we going to do?" cried Holly.

Suddenly the window-pane shattered with a great CRASH! The curtains flew open, scattering broken glass across the room...

Chapter Four

Willow

After the window smashed, Holly and Ash locked themselves in the bathroom. They stayed awake all night, listening to the bumping in the corridors and the banging on the doors.

When the sun rose, the noises stopped.

All the curtains were torn. It looked as if someone had hit the front door with an axe. And lots of the windows were broken. She and Ash tried to tidy up. But it didn't make much difference.

When her mum and dad got back, they were very angry. And they blamed Holly. They thought she'd had a party that had gone wrong.

"But I didn't have a party!" sobbed Holly. "It was just me and Ash. Not a party."

"Who's Ash? You mean a *boy* stayed here last night?" Her dad was very angry.

"No, Ash is a girl. She is my friend."

"Where does she live, this *friend* of yours? What kind of *friend* makes this kind of mess?" Her dad was shouting now.

"Ash didn't do it! She helped me tidy up!" cried Holly.

"So who made all this mess then?" asked her mum.

"Nobody," Holly said.

"What do you mean, nobody?" demanded her dad. "It didn't make itself, did it?"

Holly took a deep breath. "I think it was a ghost."

"What are you talking about?" It was her mum's turn to shout. "Have you been taking drugs?"

"You don't understand," wailed Holly. "There were lots of ghosts!"

"Oh, you can see ghosts, can you?" said her mum in a nasty voice. She didn't believe Holly.

Holly tried to explain to her parents what had happened. But she knew it sounded stupid.

Her dad thought the protestors had attacked the house again and wanted to put in CCTV cameras.

Her mum thought Holly was lying about having a party.

Holly was grounded. They took away her phone and told her she couldn't see Ash.

Her dad spent the day boarding up the broken windows. Holly sat in her room. She was sure it was ghosts that she and Ash had heard.

She was just putting a big poster of *The Blair Witch Project* on the wall above her bed when she heard something tapping on her window. It was Will. He was hanging on to the drainpipe.

"Can I come in?" he said with a grin.

Holly opened the window.

"What do you want?" she said, as quietly as she could. "My dad will kill you if he finds you here."

Will jumped into the room. "We just wanted to know that you're OK," he said. "Ash told me about last night."

Holly nodded. "My dad thinks it was the protestors. You can't stay here. He'll blame you."

"I know who it was," Will said.

"Who?"

"The trees," he said. "From the orchard."

"But they've all been chopped down," said Holly.

"It was the ghosts of the orchard," Will told her.

"Don't be silly. Trees can't turn into ghosts!" said Holly.

"I thought you believed in ghosts?" said Will.

"I do," Holly said. "But people come back as ghosts. Not trees!"

"How do you know?" asked Will. "Have you ever seen a ghost?"

"No, but – "

BANG!

Holly and Will both jumped. Someone was knocking on the bedroom door.

The door-handle started to turn. They froze.

"Holly? Are you in there?" called her mum.

"Yes, Mum. I'll be down in a minute," said Holly

""Did I hear you talking to someone?" asked her mum

"No... I'm just talking to myself," Holly replied. She tried not to giggle.

When she heard her mum walk away, she said, "You've got to go," and pushed Will towards the window.

"OK," Will said. "But listen. The trees are angry. I don't think you should stay here tonight. It's not safe. You've got to get out of here."

Will turned to climb onto the window-sill.
And then he turned back, and kissed her.

Chapter Five

Timber!

BANG!

Holly sat up in bed. Someone was knocking very loudly on the front door. She was very scared.

It was starting again! Will was right.

Holly ran down the corridor and burst into her parent's bedroom. Her mum looked like she had seen a ghost. Her dad was trying to ring the police.

"It's those stupid protestors again!" he growled. "And I can't get a signal."

"What's that smell?" asked Holly. "Apples?"

"Smells like pears to me," said her mum. "No, cherries."

Outside they could hear the angry whispers of the wind. Then the tapping on the windows began. Quietly at first, then louder and louder.

The banging on the front door went on and on. Then the floorboards began to creak and groan. Something was coming up the stairs.

Holly's dad looked round for a weapon. Her mum hid under the bed clothes.

The bedroom door-handle started to turn. The door rattled.

The tapping on the window grew louder and louder. Suddenly the window pane burst with a CRASH! A huge tree branch fell into the room. They all screamed at the same time.

"Look at the door!" shouted Holly.

A long green spiral of ivy was crawling under the bedroom door.

It curled round one of the legs of the bed. More ivy was coming in through the broken window. The paintwork on the walls was cracking.

More branches burst into the room. They could hear tiles sliding off the roof. The whole house was shaking now.

BANG!

BANG!

BANG!

"What's happening?" shouted Holly's mum.

"It's the trees!" Holly shouted back. "They're cutting down the house!"

A large branch grabbed her dad's ankle.
He yelped. Another branch gripped his arms.
They were pulling him towards the window.

He held on to the bed but the branches were too strong. A long finger of ivy was round his throat.

"Do something, Holly! Do something!" wailed her mum.

Her dad was trying to say something. But he couldn't speak. The ivy was choking him to death.

Holly looked round the room. A box of matches!

She picked up the box and tried to light a candle. Her hands were shaking. She kept dropping the matches.

"Hurry!" screamed her mum.

Holly lit a candle. She held the flame to the ivy.

The ivy hissed like an angry nest of green snakes. She threw the candle into the tree branches and they burst into flames.

Her dad fell to the floor, rubbing his throat and gasping for breath. His arms were badly burnt. The room was now full of smoke and fire.

"Quick!" yelled Holly. "We've got to get out!"

She pushed her parents towards the door. The corridors and stairs were covered in ivy. And the ivy was moving.

Leaves grabbed at their legs as they ran past. Small branches stabbed at them. Sharp twigs scratched their faces.

They could feel the heat of the fire as it ran through the top floors.

Holly jumped the last few stairs and ran out into the garden. Her parents were just behind her.

Roof-tiles were falling to the ground. The air was full of burning branches and sparks. They carried on running until they reached the road.

When they turned round, the night sky was lit by the flames from the house. Somewhere in the distance they could hear sirens.

Holly shivered. Her mum put her arm round her shoulder.

The burning house swayed in the midnight air. And then with a groan of pain, the old house fell to the earth like a great tree.

Chapter Six

Roots

Holly walked through the village, enjoying the morning sun. She had never been to Ash's house before. But Ash had said that she and Will lived at the other end of the village, next to the shop.

Holly hadn't seen her friends since the fire. And now she had to say goodbye.

She and her mum were leaving as soon as her dad got better. He had spent the last few days in the hospital and he was going to be off work for at least a month. They were going to rent a house in the city until he was better.

The local council planned to buy the old orchard land and turn it into a park.

She reached the bridge at the end of the village. There were no more houses here, just fields. She must have passed Ash's house without seeing it.

She turned round and walked back. There was the village shop. But where was the house? She went into the shop.

"Excuse me," she said, "I'm looking for two friends of mine. They live here somewhere. A boy and a girl." Holly didn't know their surname. "The girl is very tall and she's called Ash. And her brother is called Willow."

The old man behind the counter shook his head. "Sorry, miss. There's nobody called that round here."

This made no sense. Of course they lived here.

Holly went outside. She stood on the bridge. Some ducks were swimming on the river. There were no houses near the shop, just a field.

And two tall trees, waving in the warm sunshine.

Drawing a Veil

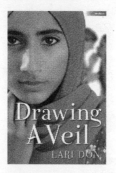

Ellie and Amina are best friends. But when
Amina decides to start wearing the hijab, it
attracts the attention of the bullies. Does it
matter if best friends have different beliefs?
A thought-provoking story about friendship,
culture and modern life.

ISBN 978-1-4081-5559-2
RRP £5.99

Zero to Hero

Will is football mad, but he's the shortest
boy in the year, and one of the slowest. He
knows his skills at passing and ball control
could make up for his lack of size, but the
team coach is looking for fast players. Will he
ever get a chance to show what he can do?

ISBN 978-1-4081-5560-8
RRP £5.99

Pitch Dark

David wants to be on the school team, like he was before. But Nick, the current goalie, has killed off any hope of that. Walking home one night, David meets a stranger who will change his life forever. But will David's football dream turn into a living nightmare?

ISBN 978-1-4081-5573-8
RRP £5.99